BUZZY BEAR

Library of Congress Catalog Card Number: 63-10830

Printed in the United States of America
by Polygraphic Company of America.

IN THE GARDEN

by DOROTHY MARINO

FRANKLIN WATTS, INC.
575 Lexington Avenue, New York 22

One nice sunny morning,
Mother Bear was busy
cleaning house.
Buzzy Bear felt hungry.
"May I get a cookie
from the cupboard?"
he asked Mother Bear.
"Go ahead,"
said Mother Bear.

Buzzy
climbed
up to the
cupboard
and got
a cookie.

When he climbed down from the cupboard,
Buzzy was in such a hurry
that he jumped right into Mother Bear's mop pail!

What a splash!

Mother Bear said,
"Perhaps you'd better go out
and help your father in the garden."

Buzzy ran out to the garden.
Father Bear was on his knees,
patting the loose ground.

"May I help garden?" asked Buzzy.
"Why, yes," said Father Bear.

Buzzy picked up the rake
and started raking
where Father Bear
had patted the ground.

"No! No!" cried Father Bear.
"I've just planted seeds there.
You can get the sprinkler
and sprinkle them with water."

Buzzy got the sprinkler
and sprinkled water around the garden.

"No! No!" cried Father Bear. "Not there.
Those are weeds.
We just pull them up."
Father Bear pulled up some weeds.
"Like this," he said.

Buzzy put down the sprinkler
and pulled up some plants.

"No! No!" shouted Father Bear.
"Those are flowers.
We just pick them."
Father Bear carefully picked a flower.
"Like this," he said.

Buzzy carefully picked
some little flowers
from a pepper plant.

"No! No!" shouted Father Bear.
"Leave those flowers.
They'll turn into peppers."

"We'll cover the pepper plants tonight
because it's going to be very cold,"
said Father Bear.
He put a covering over a pepper plant.
"Like this," he said.

"It's going to be very cold tonight,"
Buzzy said to a woodchuck
who was nibbling in the garden.
"You'll need a blanket."

Father Bear stopped beside Buzzy again.
"I didn't put a pepper plant here," he said.

He lifted up the cover
and there was the woodchuck.

"Shoo! Shoo!" shouted Father Bear.

"We don't cover up woodchucks, Buzzy.
We chase them out of the garden."
Father Bear waved the cover at the woodchuck.
"Like that," he said.

A bird hopped into the garden.
"Shoo! Shoo!" shouted Buzzy,
and he chased the bird out.

"No! No!" cried Father Bear.
"We don't chase birds out.
They help us get rid of insects."

Buzzy sat down beside the garden to think.
He watched Father Bear awhile.

Then Buzzy got the sprinkler again.
He sprinkled water on the new garden.

He pulled a weed.

He picked a flower.

He covered a pepper plant.

He chased the woodchuck.

And he smiled at the bird
who hopped into the garden.

Father Bear watched Buzzy Bear.
"Now, that's what I call a good gardener," he said.
Buzzy's eyes shone when Father Bear said that.

Then Buzzy picked some more flowers
and marched right into the house,
and gave them to Mother Bear.